The Trap

A Richard Jackson Book

The Trap

Marc Talbert

A DK INK BOOK

DK PUBLISHING, INC.

A Richard Jackson Book

Ink

DK Publishing, Inc.
95 Madison Avenue
New York, New York 10016

Visit us on the World Wide Web at http://www.dk.com

Library of Congress Cataloging-in-Publication Data
Talbert, Marc [date]
The trap / Marc Talbert
p.   cm.
"A DK Ink book."
"A Richard Jackson Book."
Summary: Ellie's attempt to avenge her cat, Bob, who has been killed and eaten by a marauding coyote, backfires when the trap she sets injures a neighborhood dog, thus heightening her awareness of life, death, and nature's way.
ISBN: 0-7894-2599-8
[1. Coyotes—Fiction. 2. Cats—Fiction. 3. Dogs—Fiction.] I. Title.
PZ7.T14145Tr   1999   98-35541
[Fic]—dc21   CIP   AC

Book design by Liney Li
The text of this book is set in 12 point Meridien Roman.
Printed and bound in U.S.A.

First Edition, 1999

2   4   6   8   10   9   7   5   3   1

For
Hollis Hassenstein

and
in memory of Clorox
a crazy, wonderful cat

Chapter 1

The cool, early morning air slid through the cracked-open window, feathering Ellie under the chin, tickling. She smiled in her sleep.

The window rattled as the breeze sighed. A single note came with it, flutelike, but loud enough to make Ellie stir.

Drowsy yet curious, hugging her pillow, not wanting to let go of sleep, she turned her face toward the window and opened an eye as the note swelled. The sun exploded up from the mountains in the east and, at the same moment, the sound shattered into many sharp notes.

Coyotes! Ellie sat up, wide-eyed, hugging her pillow tighter. They yipped and barked across the ridge by the house. Crazy as floodwaters, their song plunged down the arroyo's gullet, disappearing into the earth's belly.

Ellie slammed the window shut. The sound of coyotes made her tremble. It was a beautiful sound, but taunting—as if the coyotes couldn't help bragging, laughing about all the animals they'd killed and eaten during the night. The sound of coyotes made her feel as if her stomach had sucked up her gut like a spaghetti noodle.

It was time to get dressed and eat breakfast before the school bus came. Instead, Ellie flopped back onto her bed and pulled the covers to her chin. She wanted to recapture the sweet, slow softness of waking. She let herself melt into the growing warmth under the covers for as long as she dared.

Just as she was about the throw off her covers,

Bob jumped onto her bed, purring. He padded from her stomach to her chest and hopped over her face, his underfur making her nose tingle. He placed a paw on her head and, firmly but gently, bared his claws to hold her still. Swallowing his purr, he began to groom her, flattening a patch of her hair with his rough tongue. He scraped at her scalp through her wet hair.

Ellie lay still, knowing his claws would draw blood if she moved. Bob took this job seriously. Even though he was her age, at times he treated her as if she were a kitten. If she didn't cooperate, then he punished her with his claws. Ellie closed her eyes, listening to his tongue on her skin, thinking of a scrub pad on a frying pan.

When he slowed down, she sat up and scooped him into her arms. He went limp. He purred as Ellie scratched around the ruff that made him look like a bobcat. He purred even louder as she scratched toward the end of his backside, where he would have had a tail if he hadn't been a Manx.

"Time to get going." She set him on the floor and pushed up onto her feet.

A dog began barking outside the window. Fang? Fang was the name she'd given a gentle old mutt who roamed the neighborhood, landing at her house every so often. Only once before had she heard him bark this wildly—two weeks ago when a young bear had wandered into their yard looking for food.

She rushed from her bedroom to see what was going on. Could it be another cranky bear, stiff and hungry, waking up from its cold winter's nap?

Her parents had turned off the heat, even though it sometimes dipped below freezing at night. She wished her feet weren't bare. The hallway was frigid and so was the living room. In the kitchen, the refrigerator seemed to be shivering instead of humming. She was shivering, too, more from excitement and fear than from the cold.

Ellie inched open the back door and peeked outside. Fang stopped barking. He turned to her and lifted his slobbery lips. His nubby yellow fangs and red gums would have been scary if she didn't know he was smiling. His whole body wagged.

Ellie peered beyond him. Shadows were fast disappearing as the sun rose. She saw her father's pickup next to the shed. Her mother's car was gone—she must have been called to the hospital to help deliver a baby. Everything looked ordinary. Nothing looked like a bear.

Ellie shrugged at Fang. He sat now, his tail twitching back and forth as if nothing were wrong.

"Silly dog," she said, opening the door to let him inside.

Fang had just settled under the table when Bob

sashayed across the kitchen. He sniffed Fang's rear before stepping over his hind legs, lying down, curling his back against Fang's chest. Fang sniffed Bob's ears, and Bob rolled onto a shoulder, batting gently at Fang's nose with his paw. Ellie marveled at how comfortably they got along. From Fang's first visit, not that long ago, they'd acted like old friends.

On the way to the cupboard for cereal, Ellie glanced at the fishbowl by the toaster. It needed water—Bob drank from it, the goldfish rising to the top, fascinated by Bob's tongue striking. This morning the goldfish was nosing the first fly of the season, which floated on the water. While the fly struggled, making tiny motorboat noises, the fish seemed to want to play.

Ellie was pouring milk into her bowl of cereal when she heard her father's footsteps.

She turned toward him. "Fine!" she said as he pulled a chair from the table and sat. Now she said, "Good!"

Ellie made a point of answering "How are you doing?" and "How'd you sleep?" before her mother or father could ask.

Her father yawned as he made sure the flaps of his button-down collar were fastened. "Such woofing! What's gotten into this mooching pooch, anyway?" He nudged Fang with the toe of a tassled loafer. "And those coyotes. Hear 'em?"

"Yeah," Ellie said. "They were close." Her shoulders stiffened. "On that east ridge."

Her father nodded. "I'd guess it's a new pack. Most varmints around here have been shot or trapped."

"Must of missed some." Ellie shrugged the stiffness from her shoulders as she looked at the clock. It was later than she thought. Even her father was running late this morning. "Want this?" she asked, setting her bowl on the table. He frowned at the Sugar Bangs. "I didn't touch 'em, Daddy," she said, pulling lunch things from the refrigerator.

"Fine," her father said. "They can't be good for you."

Ellie rinsed the paring knife once she'd done making her lunch and grabbed a clean glass from the dish rack. Before she poured water into the pot in the window over the sink, she noticed the shamrocks had been eaten down again. By mice, probably.

Was Bob getting too old and fat to catch them now?

Out the window, from the corner of her eye, she saw the long, yellow tube of the bus glide into view. "Good-bye!" she shouted, grabbing her jacket from its hook, and her backpack by the door.

"You forgot to brush your hair!" her father called.

As she ran, Ellie frantically ran fingers through her hair, trying to fluff it up where Bob had groomed her.

Going to school with cat-licks was more embar-rassing than going to school with cow-licks.

She climbed the steps and looked around. Beth, her best friend, wasn't on the bus.

But Troy was—and next to him was an empty seat. Ellie snagged it.

Chapter 2

Ellie couldn't remember a more miserable day—except the cold, windy day last fall when she went lake fishing with her father. The water had been choppy enough to make her seasick. Fish had been attracted to her vomit, which was the only reason she'd caught anything at all.

She'd had no such luck today. Nothing about her had seemed attractive to anybody or anything.

On the bus coming home, Reeba and Corey hadn't even looked at her as they walked past— not that she wanted to sit with them. A second-grader had slid into the seat next to hers and, before she could make him move, the bus had pulled away from the curb. According to the driver, once he'd started it was "lockdown," as if the bus were some kind of juvenile prison.

The rolling turns and bumps of the route made Ellie as seasicky as she'd been in the boat with her dad. It didn't help that the second-grader had stepped in dog doo-doo and was scraping it off onto the back of the seat in front of them. Thawed dog doo was a sure sign of spring—and of spring fever, which was making it impossible for her to concentrate on anything but not concentrating.

Or to think. The day had started so well. Ever since first grade, she'd liked Troy. He had his mother's dark Hispanic eyes and his father's Irish freckles. He'd been polite enough when she sat next to him but he didn't talk once to her, even though he talked to a lot of kids all around them.

It had been downhill from there.

There'd been a pop quiz in math. She'd meant to study last night—until she got hooked on a

TV program about a girl who discovers that her father isn't her father, who turns out to be her PE teacher who had a sex-change operation after he/she divorced her mother.

And because Beth was sick, Ellie got stuck eating lunch with Reeba and Corey, who couldn't stop giggling about how cute it was that Troy's jeans had a hole in the butt—and was that under-wear or skin showing through? And then there was rope climbing in gym, which should have been great—she could climb better than almost anybody in her class, including the boys. Instead, the boys seemed to hoot and laugh louder at her than any of the other girls as they looked up at her. What had they seen?

Stumbling off the bus, Ellie could barely wait to snuggle up with Bob and talk on the telephone with Beth.

She was surprised to find Fang waiting for her by the mailbox. He smiled at her and wagged his tail as the bus roared off.

"You crazy dog," she said, walking over to him and stroking the top of his head. She'd never liked dogs much until Fang had wandered into her life. She'd always considered herself to be a cat person.

"What are you doing, still hanging around?" she asked as he escorted her to the house. She opened the door for him, but Fang parked himself by the bottom step and turned his attention to the east ridge, beyond the garage.

Ellie remembered the coyotes she'd heard that morning. She studied the familiar backbone of dirt and rock. Were they lurking in shadows, watching and waiting? Ellie had heard stories of single coyotes luring dogs over ridge tops, only to have several coyotes ambush them for a meal on the other side. Even though he was old, Fang seemed tough and smart enough not to fall for that.

Ellie saw nothing unusual. "Suit yourself," she told Fang, and went inside.

Ellie liked the quiet of the house before her parents got home. Bob kept her company as she read or watched television or talked on the telephone. He'd sit in her lap and purr, or he'd jump onto the sofa's back and groom her hair.

Today he wound between her legs, tripping her. He meowed without stopping as she made a snack. "What's gotten into you?" she finally asked. "You want to go outside?"

She took a couple of steps toward the kitchen door and his meowing turned joyful. She stopped, remembering the coyotes.

"I can't let you out," she said. But he was already at the door, purring and rubbing up against it.

All Ellie wanted was a little peace and quiet, a chance to call up Beth, see if she was really sick or if she'd been faking. Surely Fang would look after Bob.

She opened the door and he sprang outside. The cat threw himself to the ground in front of

Fang, stretching and rolling. Fang looked from Bob to Ellie, smiling. "Thanks," she said to the dog.

Ellie dropped, sprawling, onto the sofa. "Ah," she sighed. Just as she was about to reach for the phone, she heard Fang barking, more fierce and frantic than that morning. "What next!" She jumped up and ran to the kitchen. Hand on the knob, she stared out the kitchen door's window. Breath caught in the back of her mouth.

A coyote stood by the garage, calmly staring at Fang, who continued to bark, the hair on his back spiked.

The coyote's gaze shifted upward, his amber eyes glowing. Even through the window he'd seen her. He looked beautiful and dangerous. His coat was tawny, both furry and feathery, his tail was full and fat. In one fluid motion, he lifted his leg against the garage and disappeared around the back corner.

Fang continued to bark, not moving. Why wasn't he chasing? As if in answer, Ellie saw Bob crouched between the dog's hind legs.

When she opened the door, Bob leaped between her legs and disappeared inside the house.

Fang stopped barking and looked up at her.

"Good boy," she said, her voice shaking.

She looked toward the garage, to where the coyote had been. She wouldn't have been surprised to see that his shadow had left a coyote-shaped stain on the wall. And she'd never before looked into eyes like that. They'd been as yellow as Fang's teeth. They'd been proud eyes, devilish eyes. Calm and careful. In less than a moment those eyes had almost seemed to know who she was, what she was thinking. They had challenged her, daring her to follow, knowing that she wouldn't, judging her a coward.

"Come on," Ellie said, looking back at Fang. "Let's go inside."

Chapter 3

Ellie closed the door and turned to face the kitchen. She shuddered. Her eyes wandered toward the fishbowl. The fly had stopped moving but the fish continued to stare at it, its mouth opening and closing, seeming to blow kisses to it. Ellie plucked the fly by its soggy wings and took it to the sink. Instead of throwing it down the drain she dropped it into the pot of shamrocks for fertilizer—not that it would help much with mice eating them down as fast as new leaves sprouted.

"Well," she sighed, comforted by the sound of her own voice. "That was a close one, wasn't it, Bob?"

But Bob had disappeared.

Using her most soothing tone, she called for him. She stepped into the living room and looked behind the couch. No Bob. "Come on, Bob," she pleaded. He didn't appear. She returned to the kitchen and grabbed a bowl from the cabinet and a spoon from the silverware drawer. She tapped the bowl, making a string of bell-like sounds as she struck its rim. Bob usually came trotting, expecting a treat of milk or canned cat food.

Still no Bob. "Where do you think he is?" she asked Fang. But when she looked behind her, to where Fang had been sitting, all she saw was the old, scuffed linoleum. "Come on, guys!"

She finally found Fang in her bedroom, his nose stuck under the comforter she hadn't pulled up over her bed. His tail twitched, but then he yelped and jerked out his nose.

"Hey, Bob. That isn't nice," she said, stretching alongside Fang and lifting the edge of the comforter. A paw shot out, claws showing, barely missing her hand. The next time he swiped at her, she grabbed and pulled. He tensed and then went limp.

Ellie wanted to cuddle Bob, to let him know he was safe and that everything was all right. But he was covered in dust balls. Ellie stood and took him to the kitchen to get his brush. He squirmed as she tried to arrange him on her lap. "Come *on!*" she said, thinking of how Bob expected her to act with the patient respect of a kitten when he groomed her. With a grunt, Fang flopped at Ellie's feet.

Bob seemed to be shedding more than usual, even for spring. His undercoat was as fine as lint from the clothes drier, and she pulled out clumps of it with each stroke of the brush. Had Bob's coyote scare loosened his hair? Wisps floated in the air around her, making her sneeze. Her shirt and pants were almost slippery with it when she tried to brush the hair off.

She was about finished enough to make that call to Beth when she heard a car pulling up next to the house. Fang growled but stayed under the table. It was too early to be her father. Maybe the meter reader from the electrical company? Her mother hardly ever came home early. . . .

Bob jumped off her lap as Ellie's mother flung the door open.

"What a—" her mother began, sinking into the chair next to Ellie's.

"You won't believe what happened this afternoon!" Ellie interrupted.

Her mother smiled at her with raised eyebrows. "Twins," she said, "in case you're wondering." She looked hard at Ellie. "What? What happened?"

"A coyote, right by our garage. Fang barked and it went away." Ellie picked cat hair off her jeans. "Twins? Complications?"

Her mother nodded. "But they're okay. A coyote? By the garage? Sure it wasn't a stray dog?"

"I'm sure, Mom. It had yellow eyes. Good thing Fang was here. Was it Frank McCartney's mother?"

"Yes. Identical." Ellie's mother smiled at Fang. "Good dog," she said, reaching under the table to pat him on the head. "Must have been waiting for the cat. Coyotes are smart enough to leave people alone. Was Bob outside?"

Ellie nodded. "Do you think he's safe anymore? Outside?"

"Bob's a clever cat and old enough to have learned a thing or two about surviving. It can't be the first coyote that's been around here. Usually we just don't see them. Besides," she said, getting to her feet, "I don't think that coyote will be coming back now that he knows Fang is around." Her voice trailed off as she left the kitchen, headed for the living room.

Ellie looked at Fang, who was looking up at

her, smiling. "Think you could stick around, boy? For good?"

From the corner of her eye, she saw Bob leap onto the counter and pad over to the fishbowl. Arching his neck almost like a duck, he began lapping. As usual, the fish floated up toward Bob's tongue, drawing a little closer each time it hit water.

What a day!

Ellie glanced out the kitchen window as she walked toward the telephone. Everything seemed ordinary, which made her wonder what could be hiding just beyond what she could see. She hoped Beth was well enough to at least listen.

Chapter 4

Ellie began to feel differently about the hills around her house. That afternoon they had seemed the same as always—rumpled and comfortable, with fleshy earth colors beneath the greens of the trees. Sometimes, when she was most dreamy, Ellie imagined that the hills were a sleepy tangle of children and that the thin clumps of piñon and juniper trees were really a loosely crocheted afghan draped over them. She imagined the children's bare heads and hips showing through, their shoulders and elbows, bent knees and bottoms.

But when dusk began to fall, the hills around her house rang with the yodeling of coyotes. How many were there? It was hard to tell with their songs echoing from ridge to ridge. Hearing coyotes, and looking out her bedroom window, Ellie imagined that the yipping and barking and singing caused the sleeping hills to stir. She knew it was only darkening clouds rising above them, but she imagined the hills looming taller, creeping nearer. Inky shadows spread from many hulking shoulders. And the bodies she imagined grew burly and menacing, as they shifted toward the comfortable flatness of her family's land.

Ellie felt silly imagining the hills awake and moving toward her. She felt silly to be afraid. But after seeing the coyote mark the garage she couldn't help herself. She couldn't help being afraid for Bob.

Ellie wanted to believe her mother. She wanted to believe that Bob was smart enough to know a thing or two about surviving. But Bob was acting anything except smart these days. That taste of spring had crazed him as much as chopped raw liver. He avoided his litter box, begging to go outside to dig in the softening soil of the flower beds and garden.

The day after the coyote, Fang disappeared, left for another house, maybe even his own. For several days Ellie tried to take the dog's place, to guard Bob each time she let him out. As soon as he did his thing, she scooped him up before he stopped to lick himself clean.

She'd just stepped into the kitchen, Bob struggling to be free, when the phone rang.

"For you, Ellie," her father called.

Ellie let Bob jump from her arms and rushed to her bedroom. Beth?

"Ellie?"

"Beth!" Bob must have trotted along behind her. He began weaving himself between her legs, rubbing against her, meowing, almost cater-wauling. "What's up?" Wanting to quiet him, she reached down to his head. He jumped out of reach and continued to meow.

"Had a question about math. Thought you could help."

Ellie sat at her desk and found her math text. "Which problem?" Bob jumped onto her lap. Ellie was grateful for his silence as she leafed through the pages with one hand and steadied Bob with her other. Instead of curling up or purring, he sat rigid in her lap, as if ready to pounce. Then, without warning, he began kneading her thighs with his claws.

"Ouch!" Ellie cried, pushing the cat onto the floor. A claw caught on her jeans and hung him up for a moment.

"What's going on?"

"Nothing!" Ellie hadn't meant to sound angry. "Bob!"

"Look. You don't—"

"I don't believe it! He was sharpening his claws on my leg!"

"Oh." Beth laughed, sounding relieved. "Maybe you should get him declawed."

"Yeah, except that he might need them to protect himself from coyotes." Bob jumped up on her lap again. Ellie glared at him, and he seemed to glare up at her, his ears back. "Which problem?"

Before Beth could say, Bob began to knead Ellie's thighs, more vigorously this time.

"Hey!" she shouted.

"What?"

"Not you!" Ellie said, throwing Bob off a second time. "It's Bob. I think I'm bleeding."

Beth laughed, then stopped. "Sorry," she apologized, "but your problem seems worse than mine. Maybe I should call you later."

"Yeah," Ellie said, watching Bob tear at a mat of hair on his shoulder with his teeth. "I'll feed him and call you back."

Bob followed her to the kitchen. His meowing grew more excited the closer they got.

Opening a can of cat food, Ellie looked out the window over the sink. The sun was setting, the sky glowing red and pink and orange and yellow. The hills seemed on fire.

She set the bowl of cat food on the floor and called into the living room. "Mom! Dad! Look at the sunset!"

"Coming!" her mother answered from the living room.

Ellie opened the door, wanting to step outside, to be part of what she saw.

A streak shot by her feet and down the steps, into darkness.

"Bob!" she shrieked. "Bob! Come back here!"

She couldn't see him, as if he'd sunk into the pooling shadows.

Close by, a lone coyote yipped from somewhere in the darkness by the garage.

Ellie ran back inside for a flashlight, almost crashing into her mother.

"Bob!" she cried. "He's disappeared! And there's a coyote out there! By the garage!"

She ran to the drawer where her parents kept the flashlights. She grabbed one and pushed the switch. Dead. She grabbed another one. Dead.

"Don't we have one that works?" Ellie was frantic now.

"Darren!" her mother called. "Know where we can—"

"No need to shout," Ellie's father said, walking into the kitchen. "I think there are some batteries in this drawer. Bob?" he asked, pulling out a packet of two.

Ellie nodded, her eyes tingling with unwanted tears.

"He's been cooped up most of the winter. Probably on a toot with an old girlfriend."

"But the coyote!" Ellie cried, slipping fresh

batteries into her flashlight. "I heard him. Right by the garage!"

"Then Bob's hiding somewhere," her mother said, gently. "We'll find him. Just wait and see."

Ellie stared down at Bob's bowl. He hadn't touched his food.

Chapter 5

Ellie and her parents looked everywhere they thought Bob might hide—under the car, under the budding lilac bush, up into the branches of the crab apple tree by the well house, in the garage, behind the woodpile with its strong smell of mice.

After fifteen minutes of searching and calling his name, Ellie went inside for a bowl and a spoon. She felt silly as she banged on the bowl, since Bob hadn't touched his food earlier. She continued banging anyway, banging so hard that the bowl chipped.

"Bob! Bob!" she cried. "BOB!"

Her father walked to her, put an arm around her shoulder, and took the bowl. "I don't think we'll find him until he wants to be found."

Her mother came over and took the spoon. "There's nothing more we can do right now, honey."

"But the coyote!"

"We've scared it to the next county," her father said.

"And Bob will stay put," her mother added. "Leave your window open. We will, too. He'll meow when he wants to come inside."

Ribbons of cold air streamed through her window, flapping in her face. She braced herself against the chill, pulling the covers to her chin. Wanting to be ready at a moment's notice, she hadn't changed out of her clothes. As she listened for Bob's meow, odd thoughts floated through her mind.

When Ellie called Beth back and told her about him running off, Beth had started crying, as if she felt Bob was never coming home.

"He's probably hiding," Ellie told Beth, trying to cheer herself up.

Ellie's thoughts jumped to the time, years ago, when she thought she'd lost Bob, only to find him snuggled up in the clothes hamper. He'd smelled for a couple days like her father's socks, but otherwise had been okay.

Ellie thought of the Christmas when Bob had played so hard with balls of crumpled wrapping paper and lengths of springy, curled ribbon that he'd finally collapsed on the floor panting, his tongue hanging out.

She thought of Bob settling on her chest as she read in bed, his purr lulling her to sleep.

Ellie pushed the covers to her waist, letting cold air blow away the sleepiness that threatened to overtake her. She waited as long as she could before pulling up the covers, shivering and staring at the ceiling, listening for cat noises outside. A car whizzed by on the county road. Leafless branches clicked together outside. No meowing.

The hair on the back of her arms lifted. Turning her head toward the bedroom door, she searched the shadows. Bob?

Nothing.

He'll come back, she told herself. He'll come back.

Her thumping heart seemed to rub against her breastbone, making blisters.

All the tears she'd been fighting broke through. She cried into her pillow, wanting not to wake her parents. She cried until she was wrung dry. Turning onto her back, she felt a twist of loneliness from not knowing where Bob was.

He has to be alive, she thought. He has to.

When sleep came, it came on cat feet—stealthily and softly.

The next morning, Ellie woke to the coyote's song. She leaped from bed, ready to shout the worst curses she knew. Instead, she closed her mouth and listened for a moment.

It was the same coyote she'd heard last night in the shadows by the garage. The same song. She was sure of it. But something was different.

Was that a meow she heard in his bark?

Beth waved for her as Ellie stepped onto the bus that morning.

"Did Bob come home last night?" she asked breathlessly, as Ellie sat beside her.

Ellie shook her head. She felt like crying, but her tears were all dried up.

Beth's eyes misted. "Oh, Ellie! He's got to come back!"

"Bob?" Ellie and Beth looked up at Troy's face, which was hanging over the back of the seat in front. Lester, who was next to Troy, turned to face them, too. "Who's Bob?"

"None of your beeswax!" Beth said.

At the same time, Ellie replied, "My cat."

Troy shrugged. "Cats do that. Go away. Come back."

"Not Ellie's cat!" Beth said.

Troy ignored her, keeping his eyes on Ellie.

"He's probably hiding," Ellie said, wanting to defend Bob. "There's a coyote that's been hanging around our house."

"Coyote chow!" Lester said, licking his lips.

Troy looked at Lester. "Could have been owl chow." He looked back at Ellie and Beth. "Great horned owls can carry cats, small dogs. Raccoons, even. My dad told me about a pair of great horned owls just outside town, in some old cottonwoods. People thought it was strange, them being so close in. My dad said some state wildlife people decided to study them and they got a cherry picker and peeked into the nest. Know what they found?"

Ellie shook her head.

"A pile of cute little cat collars!"

"With rhinestones!" Lester added.

"That's awful!" Beth said.

Once more Ellie felt like crying and nothing came. She'd never thought of protecting Bob from owls.

Troy nodded. "Can't do anything about owls. They're protected. But I'd love to do something about the coyotes."

"You mean kill them?"

Troy nodded again. "Only way to make sure they don't get cats. All you have to do is find the den. The rest is easy. The other day, my uncle was saying that it's whelping time for coyotes. In a week or two. When they've got pups, that's a good time to get 'em." He smiled at her. "I can borrow a trap from my uncle. And Lester got a

.22 from Santa that's itching to kill more than tin cans."

"Think she knows how to find the den?" Lester asked Troy.

"Know how?" Troy asked Ellie.

Ellie shook her head.

"Follow whatever trail has coyote scat on it. My uncle says they like to leave it right in the middle—where you're bound to notice it."

"Think she knows what scat is?" Lester asked Troy with a snicker.

"Yeah," Ellie answered for Troy. "Scat's what's in your head instead of brains."

Troy laughed and Beth giggled. Lester blushed and turned around in his seat.

Ellie stared at the back of his head, thinking that coyotes weren't the only varmints in her life.

Chapter 6

Fang was waiting for Ellie by the mailbox when she stepped off the bus that afternoon.

"Fang!" she said, rushing up to him. Maybe Bob was back! "Where is he?" She ran to the house.

"Bob!" she called. Fang followed. "Come on, Bob! I know you're around somewhere!"

Dumping her backpack on the back steps, Ellie walked around the garage, her eyes searching. Were those his ears poking up from a clump of grass? She stopped and Fang walked on, not even pausing as he passed the grass clump. Ellie watched him, holding her breath as he sniffed around a pile of scrap lumber, digging for a moment. She let it out when he walked away.

Fang began zigzagging in front of her, his nose to the ground. She followed. After a few steps she was surprised to see that she and Fang were walking along a faint trail she'd never noticed before, even though it was close to the garage. The trail headed east, toward the ridge.

A coyote trail?

Fang stopped and his tail grew still. Ellie walked up to him, to see what he was studying so carefully with his nose.

It was scat. Right in the middle of the trail, thinner than a hot dog, and pointed at both ends. Coyote scat?

"Hey!" she said when Fang lifted his leg. The squirt missed.

Ellie leaned over the scat. It was like a dog's,

but different. And something about it troubled her. Looking closer, she saw that it was mostly hair, matted and pressed together with bits of grass. And the hair was exactly the color of Bob's.

Ellie dropped to her knees and, swallowing down her disgust, picked the scat up, pulling some hair from it. She rolled the hair between her thumb and pointing finger. Plucking more, she tried telling herself it wasn't Bob's. But the more she touched it and studied it, the more it felt and looked like what she had brushed from Bob's coat so often.

Blinking back angry tears, Ellie looked up to see Fang nosing around in the skirt of pine needles beneath a piñon tree. She put the bits of Bob's hair in her jacket pocket and walked toward him. Fang was concentrating so hard that he didn't notice her until she touched his back. His tail jerked, twitching, and then began to wag as he stepped away from what he was sniffing.

It took Ellie a few moments to realize what she was looking at.

Teeth. In a horseshoe shape. At either end were miniature molars, set in dull and shrinking gums. At the top was a bowed line of five or six teeny-tiny teeth. On either end of these were incisors, so shiny they looked wet. Pale skin stretched across the horseshoe shape, with ridges like those she felt on the top of her own mouth. Under the teeth was a shell of bone.

Ellie took this scrap of animal into her hand. It was the right size and shape to have belonged to a cat. To Bob.

It was then she knew—deep down in the aching pit of her stomach—that Bob would never come home.

Fang sniffed at what she held. His tongue darted out, giving the bone a quick lick. He looked up at her, unsmiling, his tail not moving. Ellie dropped to her knees, threw her arms around his neck, and wept.

At dinner that night, Ellie was so quiet her mother finally asked, "Honey, are you feeling well?"

Ellie looked up from her plate, startled. "I . . . I was just thinking . . . thinking about . . . about . . ."

"About Bob?" her father asked.

She began nodding and then shook her head. "I . . . I think I found him . . . over by the ridge . . . found what's left of him."

"I was afraid of that," said her father.

"Baby!" Her mother held out her arms. Just as she had when she was little, Ellie huddled in her mother's lap. Her father pulled his chair close and held her hands in his, rubbing her palms with his thumbs.

"Fang found it. It was . . . it looked like some kind of poop on a trail," she said in a small voice.

"But it was hair. Bob's hair. And then," her voice cracked, and she felt her insides simmering, "I found the top of his mouth . . . with the skin and his gums and his teeth."

Her gut began to boil. Sobs rolled up, scalding her throat. She let herself be rocked in her mother's arms.

When she was quiet, her mother spoke in a husky voice. "Before you, I helped deliver many babies. And when I did, I thought only of helping bring life into the world. But when you were born, Ellie, when I held your slippery body against my chest, then I knew . . . knew deep in my bones . . . that your father and I had not only given you life, but death . . . your own and ours and many others besides. Only then did it hit me that my tears of joy were also tears of sorrow . . . for everything that would hurt you by dying. Honey, Bob was part of the joy. Now he's part of the sorrow. They go together."

"It's a hard thing to learn," her father said, his voice rough. "But it's part of growing up."

Ellie found herself tensing, wanting to shout, "Then I don't want to grow up!"

Instead, she tried to smile, and wiped tears from her cheek with the palm of her hand. Tomorrow, she promised herself, she'd find the den. She'd find the den and make that coyote sorry it had ever been born.

Chapter 7

Ellie dreamed about coyotes.

Their howling and yipping and yodeling and barking bounced around inside her head. They seemed to be running in circles, braiding their voices, tangling her thoughts.

She wished them all horrible deaths.

She imagined one coyote crumpled on the ground, writhing. She imagined one of Bob's bones, broken and sharp, grinding away inside the coyote's stomach or intestines or throat. It opened its mouth, and blood bubbled out.

She imagined another coyote looking over its

shoulder just as a pack of snarling dogs piled on top of it. It didn't have a chance to cry out.

She imagined a third coyote wobbling as it stood, its tongue hanging long and dry. A raven swooped down, landed on its head, and plunged its beak into an eye.

And the coyote voices went silent, one by one. One by one, the songs disappeared.

Except for the last.

She recognized its song. It was the coyote that called out the night Bob disappeared.

She woke with a start. What she was hearing was not a dream coyote. It was real. Ellie sat up and looked out the window. The sun was gathering strength to rise above the mountaintops. One last coyote cry tumbled off the ridge, down the cliff of its flank, and fell silent.

It would be impossible now to sleep in on this Saturday morning. She got up and dressed. She tiptoed past her parents' bedroom and heard steady breathing. She walked to the kitchen, grabbed a couple of cheese sticks from the refrigerator, and slipped outside.

She almost tripped over Fang, who was sacked out on the doormat. He got up, stretched, and shook. "Same to you!" Ellie whispered. Fang sat and looked up at her, his tail uncertain.

It was tempting to think of Fang keeping her company as she looked for the coyote den. He might be able to sniff his way to the den more quickly than she could find it on her own. And she'd feel safer with him nearby. But what if Fang took off after a coyote? She'd never be able to keep up and, besides, a coyote would never lead a dog to its den.

Ellie patted Fang on the head and opened the kitchen door. "Want a treat?" she asked, ushering him inside. He followed her and she peeled plastic off one of her cheese sticks. "Don't make yourself too much at home," she said, handing it to him. Her parents wouldn't be happy to find Fang alone inside, but what else could she do? As he began to chow down, she rushed outside.

It didn't take long to find the spot where Fang had discovered the scat and the roof of Bob's mouth. She set off toward the ridge, the trail narrow and faint in the early light, bending only once to avoid dropping into an arroyo.

The sun popped up, making long shadows, drawing the freshness from the night air. The landscape seemed to flatten, to go stale.

The trail up the flank of the ridge, Ellie thought, must have been made by the small feet of deer or coyotes. Her bigger feet slipped in the crumbly dirt. Rounding the prow of the ridge, she saw a hole in the hillside looking to the south, as if it were an eye set over a cheek of clay. The hair on her arms rose. Above, on the ridge top, stood the coyote she'd seen by the garage. He stared down at her. Each tawny hair glowed, as if from the same power that lit his yellow eyes.

She held her breath, tensing, expecting him to leap. Perhaps he would attack if she showed fear by retreating. Just when she felt that her lungs would burst, the coyote's head turned at something he'd heard behind him. He disappeared so quickly it seemed he'd vanished into the air.

She let out her breath, sounding like an unknotted balloon let go. She'd found the den. But she'd been seen.

Her fingers trembling, she pulled the remaining cheese stick from her pocket and peeled it. Smashed and soft and greasy, it clung to the plastic. She put it on the ground, wishing it were laced with poison, hoping the coyote would think she meant no harm with her spying.

Ellie was expecting both of her parents to be away from the house when she got back—it was her father's Saturday at the bank and her mother's weekend at the hospital. Her mother's car was gone, but her father's truck was still parked by the shed. And Fang was parked next to the truck.

Her father was lifting a coffee mug to his lips when she and the dog came inside. His breath on the coffee made steam, which matched the mood on his face.

Before her father could say anything, Ellie reached down and patted Fang's head. "Sorry," she said. "Guess I forgot to let him out." She tried to smile. Her father set down the mug.

"Young lady, where have you been?"

Ellie didn't like being talked to this way.

"Outside," she said, her voice frosty.

"Just when did you leave this house? And what in the blazes were you doing out there?"

She stared back at him. What was he getting at? What did he think she'd been doing?

"Don't give me the runaround, young lady! When I ask you a question, I expect an answer."

"Why are you talking to me like that? I'm not

a little kid. . . ." She clenched her jaw to keep from crying.

"You may think you know enough to do whatever you want without letting us know, young lady, but that's not the case. I'm late enough to work as it is. You're grounded today. I expect you to be here, in the house, every time I call you. And when we get back home, your mother and I will expect some straight answers."

Ellie could still hear the sound of her father's truck charging down the driveway as she picked up the telephone book. She jotted down a number and dialed.

"May I speak with Troy?" she asked. She smarted, listening to the television in the background. A cartoon roadrunner was beeping as a cartoon coyote tried to kill it in one complicated way or another. She heard an explosion and pictured the charred coyote standing for a moment with sad, defeated eyes before crumbling into a pile of ash. Yes! she thought.

"Hello?"

"Troy?"

"Yeah."

"Hi. This is Ellie. I think I found the coyote den."

"Yeah?"

"Yeah."

"Great! I'll get a trap from my uncle and come on over this afternoon. You can help me set it."

"Can't," Ellie said. "My dad . . . I gotta stick around the house today. Help out. You know."

"Tomorrow?"

"Don't know."

"Me neither," Troy said. "Look. I'll bring the trap to school on Monday, in my backpack. After school I'll get off at your bus stop instead of mine. I'll tell my mom I'm going to Lester's. Then I can walk home from your place in time for dinner. Got any good bait?"

"Like what?"

"Any kind of meat'll do," Troy said. "The female's probably had her pups or she's about to. She needs the most food now, at the tail end of winter, when there's not much for her or the male to catch."

"I'll get something," Ellie said. "See you. After school. Monday."

"See ya!"

When Troy hung up, Ellie looked down at Fang, who was sitting at her feet, looking up at her.

"You won't tell on me, will you, boy?" She patted him on the head. But for good measure, she fetched him a slice of old, graying lunch meat from the refrigerator.

Chapter 8

Ellie knew in her head that Bob was dead, but he was alive in her heart. All that Saturday he sprang into her thoughts the way he used to jump into her lap.

She thought of him when she showered that morning, lathering up the shampoo he preferred that she use—the others must have made her hair taste nasty. After, her damp hair chilled her. Putting on her favorite sweater, she found herself picking Bob's hair from it. She almost cried as she put the hair in an envelope for safekeeping.

Fang stuck close to her. Still, the house felt

empty without Bob. Ellie would often start saying something to him and then would talk to Fang instead. It wasn't the same. She never realized how much she'd talked to Bob before. She could have used him now, to talk about how her father had spoken to her this morning. Bob had always listened better than anyone else, including Beth. Pouring her heart out to Fang didn't seem right. They didn't know each other well enough.

There were moments when the house felt as spooky as a classroom without kids. And it felt as lonely as getting the answering machine message each time she called Beth—which Ellie did seven times. Where could she have gone off to? Who was she with?

Ellie tried reading. But she kept expecting Bob to jump into her lap and couldn't concentrate. Watching television wasn't any better. TV and stroking Bob had always gone together, and Fang curled up on the floor, just beyond reach of her feet.

Her father called her four times during the day. The last time was about three in the afternoon. "I'll be home a little early today, Ellie. We'll go into town and meet your mother after she gets off work. Thought the three of us could go to Broken Butte Bistro." Her father sounded tired.

"Sure." She tried not to seem excited, but the Broken Butte was her favorite place to eat.

"Hey, I'm sorry about this morning," he said.

"That's okay." But she could hear herself pouting.

"I don't blame you for being angry," her father said. "It's just that your mom and I are realizing how old you're getting, and it's taken us by surprise." Ellie pictured her father sitting in his red leather chair. His desk was probably clean except for folders filled with papers neatly stacked in front of him. He wasn't the kind of person who liked surprises in his work or at home.

When she didn't say anything, he cleared his throat. "I see so many girls not much older than you with tattoos in the strangest places and with pierced noses and eyebrows and lips. And just last night your mother was telling me about the pregnant girls she's seeing at work, some of them about your age, one even younger."

"Oh," she said. This was news to her father? Off the top of her head, she could come up with four or five candidates among the girls she knew.

"It's a dangerous world out there," he said. "A lot more dangerous than it should be."

It just popped out. "I'm not a cat and the boys at school aren't coyotes." There was silence at the other end, and then a sigh.

"I know, honey. I know. Look. You know how badly I feel about Bob. It's hard to see you hurting so much. And I'm sorry I let it get to me this morning. Let's put it behind us."

"Well . . ." she said, wishing her father had talked to her face-to-face instead of on the phone. "See you later," she said and, as punishment, she hung up before he had a chance to say good-bye.

On Monday, kids on the bus hooted and made kissing noises as Troy stepped off at Ellie's stop. She frowned, wanting to yell, to tell them all to shut up. But that would only make things worse.

As the bus pulled away, she saw curious faces looking at them from the windows. Beth waved. Lester's puckered lips were smashed against the back window. She hoped he was catching a nasty disease.

Ellie turned her back to the bus and was relieved to see that Fang wasn't waiting for her at the mailbox.

"Got the bait ready?" Troy asked.

"Sure," she answered and rushed into the house, not inviting him in. She was tempted to grab a snack for the two of them but decided against it. She didn't want him to get any ideas. Instead, she grabbed a package of hot dogs and ran outside. "Will these work?"

Troy nodded. "Where to?"

They followed the coyote trail, not saying anything until they came to some scat.

"Yep. Coyote." Troy bent over it. "Looks like it's been eating apples."

"Apples?"

Troy nodded. "Last year's. From the ground around Montoya's orchard, probably."

Ellie looked closer. The scat looked as if the apples had barely been chewed before being swallowed, and then had been cooked instead of digested as they wound through the coyote's guts.

"How much farther to the den?" Troy asked.

She pointed. "Just around that bend."

"We should set it around here. Don't want to spook 'em. If we do, they'll abandon the den."

Ellie thought of seeing the coyote on the ridge

the other day as Troy set down his backpack, unzipped it, and reached inside. Had she spooked it? She hoped not, because she wanted that coyote dead.

Troy pulled out a rusty-looking contraption of folded metal loops.

"What are these?" Ellie pointed to two thick strips of metal, both bent into skinny U-shapes. They were on either side of the trap and Troy held them like handles.

"Wings."

Was he joking?

Whatever they were, between them was an arch of two metal strips pressed against each other. "And these?"

"The teeth." Ellie didn't see teeth. She saw lips.

Troy pointed underneath the teeth, where there was a round disk of metal on a stem. "And this is the . . ."

"That's okay," Ellie interrupted. It looked to

her like the trap's tongue and that's what she wanted it to be.

Troy grunted and pulled out a length of chain and a stake. "Get me a rock? To pound in the stake?" Ellie looked down and saw one near her feet. She bent sideways and picked it up.

Troy looped the chain around one of the handle/wings and ran the stake through the two end chain rings, pinning them together. Just off the trail, with the heal of his shoe, he dug a shallow pit about the size of a dinner plate. Resting the trap next to this pit, he stepped on the handle/ wings. The teeth flopped open, forming a circle of metal, still looking to Ellie like lips. The "tongue" sat in the center of this circle. Most likely its real name was mechanical, impersonal. Ellie looked at the trap. What kind of damage could it do? She wanted that trap to *taste* blood!

Troy poked a finger under a "lip," trying to nudge a sliver of metal into the hook on the edge of the tonguelike thing. When his finger began to tremble, Ellie looked up. Sweat was beaded on his forehead, and his tongue was clenched between his teeth.

He's scared! she thought.

Carefully, Troy stepped off the trap. Ellie squinted, deciding that the sliver of metal on the tongue kept it all from snapping shut. Amazing, she thought.

"That'll hold." Troy's voice was taut.

Gingerly, he lifted the trap and, straight-armed, set it in the pit, gently brushing a film of dirt over it.

He held out his hand. "Hot dogs." Ellie opened the packet and handed him two. He set pieces of them just beyond the trap.

"Let's pound in the stake and get outta here," he said. "That hot dog should smell strong enough to cover up our scent." He popped a piece in his mouth and smiled.

As they rounded the garage, Ellie saw her mother's car parked by the kitchen door. Ellie pulled Troy back, behind the garage.

"My mother," she whispered. "She's home early."

Troy grinned. "Don't want her to get the wrong idea, do we."

Ellie shook her head.

"Gotcha. I'll use the coyote highway to go home."

Ellie watched Troy backtrack toward the ridge and then, with a coyotelike laugh, disappear into the arroyo.

Chapter 9

"Call me later," Beth shouted as Ellie walked to the front of the bus.

"I will," she yelled over her shoulder, stepping off.

"Hey! Don't forget to check," Troy called through his open window. He waved as the bus took off.

She ignored him. What was he doing? After yesterday, a few people had teased her about her new "boyfriend." Troy? Boyfriend? She thought about his freckles and his dark brown eyes. He was cute. Still . . .

She turned toward her house and saw Fang waiting, wagging from head to tail.

"Howdy," she said, her voice flat. Of all the days for him to show up, he'd have to pick this one. She'd need to leave him in the house again to keep him from following, and hope her parents didn't get home first. Using a voice she saved for talking with three-year-olds, Ellie asked, "Want a treat?"

As she opened the kitchen door, he sat. "Want a cookie?" He smiled, but didn't budge.

She stepped inside. "Come on, come on, come on," she coaxed. "Here. Let me show you." She went to get a sugar cookie from the cookie jar.

All set to lure him inside, she opened the door again. He was gone. Ellie nibbled at the cookie. How had he known she was trying to trick him?

Ellie took a roundabout way to the trap. She didn't want the coyotes to see her. She joined the trail a few yards beyond the trap, stopped, and stared.

What she saw near it didn't look like pieces of hot dog.

She stepped closer.

The hot dog was gone. Instead, she saw scat. More apple scat. Some kind of coyote joke.

She glanced at her watch. If she hurried, she might have time to fetch more hot dogs and rebait the trap before her parents got home.

She heard panting. Looking up, she saw Fang loping along the trail, his tail wagging, headed right for the trap.

"No!" Ellie lurched forward, waving her arms in warning.

Fang's lope broke as he dodged, stepping with his left rear foot into the center of the trap.

The sky seemed to suck in its breath. Ellie shrieked as Fang shot into the air, howling with pain and rage. He was jerked to the ground by the chain tether and landed on his chin. He scrambled up, snapping at the trap, his hackles spiked, blood oozing from the trap's metal lips.

"Fang!" Ellie cried, dropping to her knees, unable to take her eyes from his foot even though her stomach squeezed up bile, burning her throat. He was making a sound Ellie had never heard before—a combination of growling and barking and whining and crying. Strings of spit dangled from his jowls, stretching thin before breaking off. As he tore at the trap, the spit turned pink and then bright red from the gash he'd cut in his mouth. He jumped again, baring his teeth in fury, and Ellie was horrified to see that he'd ripped out one of his incisors. He yelped as the tether yanked him back, onto the side of his face.

"Fang!" she cried again. Scrambling to her feet, she threw herself onto his shoulders to keep him from struggling, to keep him from hurting himself more.

Roaring, he turned on her, his eyes savage as he caught the sleeve of her jacket in his teeth.

Ellie screamed at the sound of ripping cloth, but held on.

She clung to him, thinking she'd gone blind and deaf in the silence that followed. The searing of trapped tears seemed to weld her eyelids together. She struggled to open them. Fang whimpered as she loosened her hold, and then he began to tremble. His eyes were wild, but beginning to glaze. Ellie didn't know if he was looking at her or through her.

She slowly let go, not wanting to spook him. The ground on which she knelt looked bruised where blood and spit had fallen. She forced herself to look at the trap. The metal was slick with blood, looking like clown lips clenched in a tight smile. Ellie saw only a sliver of space between the lips. And skin was bunched up around his paw like a fallen sock. Was Fang's foot hanging by no more than a shred?

"It's okay, Fang." She tried to sound calm, but her voice quavered and she spoke louder than she intended. "Let me get this thing off you and we'll see what's what."

She placed a palm over one of the trap's handles. As careful as she was trying to be, Fang cried out. Startled, she drew her hand back.

"I'm only trying to help!" The words struggled to squeeze through her throat. She reached again with both hands, trying to loosen the lips. Ellie leaned with her full weight, grunting, her nose almost touching Fang's pulpy leg.

The trap quivered with her effort and began to relax but the lips refused to flop open.

"Come on!" she cried. Jumping up, she placed both feet where Troy had stepped while setting it.

The lips flopped open, bloodied and gruesome. But Fang didn't move. Instead, he looked up at her, his eyes twitching.

"You gotta move," she groaned. When he didn't, she pushed him onto his side. The trap began to slip from under her feet, moving as if it were alive, preparing to strike again. She jumped away, the trap kicking up dirt as it snapped shut.

"Jeez!" she gasped.

Fang lay panting, dirt becoming mud beneath his wound. Ellie didn't know what to do. Would he be able to walk to her house? If he couldn't, would she be able to carry him?

"Come on, Fang." She crawled over to him. "Let's go home."

The old dog lifted his head as if struggling to sit. "Attaboy." She steadied him as he pushed himself up with his front legs until he was sitting. "Good boy." Propped up, he nosed around his wound and began to lick it. Each time his tongue touched it, the foot flopped in a way that made Ellie flinch. Between licks, he whined like a small puppy.

Ellie couldn't bear to watch. She slid her fingers over his shoulders. He didn't seem to know she was touching him, but it made her feel better.

She stroked lightly, afraid she might nudge him off balance.

Ellie let her eyes flick to the top of the ridge. She searched for relief in the soothing blue of the sky. She tensed.

What she saw was not a rock, but was as still as one.

Chapter 10

The coyote stood above them, watching. Was he enjoying Fang's pain? Was he waiting to call his family for dinner?

He didn't move and seemed unconcerned that Ellie was looking at him.

"Get outta here!" she shrieked. "Scram!"

The coyote slowly turned. Giving her one last, calm look, he slipped over the ridge, disappearing.

Ellie had no choice now. She had to get Fang home before the coyote came back with others. Fang was still cleaning the wound. White showed through the blood with every swipe of his tongue and she hoped it wasn't bone. But what else could it be?

"Come on, boy," she said, standing. She pulled gently on his collar, urging him to get up on his good hind leg, to move. He whined and leaned against her, as if wanting to lie down. "Come on!" She braced herself to hoist up his hindquarters. He was too heavy.

"You gotta try!" she moaned, plopping down next to him. He continued to lick his wound, and she stared into space, hoping to calm herself, hoping to collect her thoughts. She knew that if she didn't come home for dinner, her parents would come looking for her. If she could find a big stick for protection, and pile up a few rocks for throwing, she could surely hold out until then.

Shadows were growing as she looked. What about the dark? Coyotes seemed to melt into and out of shadows and the dark.

She scrambled to her feet and picked up a rock.

Close by, and behind them, the coyote cried. She spun toward the sound.

The coyote cried again, seeming closer.

"Go away!" she cried, cocking her arm, not knowing where to throw.

Fang heard the coyote's second howl. He lifted his head and stared into space with wide eyes, as if he were waking from a nightmare, as if he didn't know where he was. His eyes connected with hers and when the coyote called a third time, they began to clear.

He tried to heave up onto his feet. "Yes!" Ellie encouraged. He fell back with a grunt and panted before trying again.

When he fell back a second time, Ellie grabbed him around his shoulders. "Here," she groaned. "Try again." This time he steadied himself on his three good legs, teetering, panting hard. His body went rigid when the coyote cried out again. He tried to turn toward the sound, but his injured foot seemed to twist.

Fang's lips drew up and he cried/growled, as if something had lunged at him from behind. He leaned into her legs and, for a moment, she thought he needed her for balance. When he looked up toward the coyote, she sensed that he was putting himself between her and danger instead. Only when he seemed certain they were safe did he pull away from her and, with his nose, begin herding her down the trail.

Fang hobbled slowly, the rhythm of his panting broken by the snap of his teeth and then a squeek that could have been a mouse caught in a trap. He seemed less concerned about himself than he was about her. "Hey, cut it out!" she cried as he nudged her along. He whined whenever she slowed to extend her hand, never allowing her to slip behind him. He kept his eyes on her, as if he were determined to get her home safely.

To make it easier for him, Ellie walked around the rocks and roots, the holes and bumps. Fang grew impatient with her zigzagging, as if she were playing a silly game. He whined until she began walking down the middle of the trail.

What would she tell Troy about the trap? Should she lie? Would he want to reset it? She shuddered. What else would it catch? She looked over her shoulder at Fang. He lumbered along, hunched, blood oozing from his dangling leg, gathering until there was enough to splat on the ground.

She pictured a coyote stepping into the trap, its leg crushed like Fang's. She imagined the coyote crying in surprise and pain and fear. For the first time, this picture didn't bring her joy—didn't promise any triumph at revenging Bob's death. She thought of Fang. What would have happened if she hadn't been there to help him? How would he have endured the pain, the shock, the loss of blood, until help arrived—if it *ever* arrived.

An old song suddenly popped into her head and Ellie began to hum. She sang the words in her head, finally letting them out: "Hush-a-bye, don't you cry, all the pretty little horses. When you wake, you shall find all the pretty little horses." She glanced over her shoulder often, singing to Fang.

Ellie relaxed, continuing to sing, making up words now. It seemed to perk him up and it sure made her feel better. She was concentrating on Fang more than on the trail. Stumbling, she looked up, startled, to see the garage. Her heart leaped with fear and hope.

She ran around the back end of the garage.

Her mother's car was parked in its usual spot.

"Mom!" Ellie shrieked. "MOM!"

Chapter 11

The kitchen door opened. "Ellie?" her mother called. She was wiping her hands on a dish towel.

From behind, Ellie heard Fang cry out. "Fang!" She spun around and ran back. Fang had collapsed. She rushed up to him. "We're almost there! Come on, boy! You can do it!"

Ellie felt her mother's hand on her shoulder. She tried to keep from sobbing, but the sobs she held back became hiccups.

"He needs a vet," her mother said in her nurse voice. "And I need to turn off the oven."

■ ■ ■

Ellie sat in the backseat with Fang's head in her lap. It had taken the two of them to lift him into the car. Her shirt and jeans were growing stiff where blood had soaked in and dried. Her hands itched where blood had dried and cracked.

"The trap was set alongside a trail? By the ridge?"

Ellie nodded, meeting her mother's eyes in the rearview mirror and then veering away.

They turned onto the main road, bumping onto pavement. Fang whined. As if he were a puppy, he tried to crawl into her lap. She stroked the top of his head. "It's okay, boy," she said.

"That trap could have gotten *you! Anybody!* Was it baited?"

Ellie thought of the coyote scat where the hot dog had been. She wished she'd never *seen* the trap. She wished that she'd never agreed to let Troy set it. Instead of answering, she looked down at Fang. The top of his head was stained with his own blood where Ellie had patted him. She wondered what her mother would think if she knew Ellie had a part in setting the trap?

"Was it baited?" her mother asked again.

Ellie swallowed the truth. "No!" she blurted. As if to convince herself, she shook her head.

"What kind of trap was it? For coyotes?"

"I don't know," Ellie moaned, not wanting to be asked any more questions. Lying made her feel weak and winded.

"Who could have done such a thing?" Her mother barely paused at the first stop sign, gunning the car when she saw the intersection was clear. Ellie caught her breath and Fang whimpered.

"Do you remember where it was?"

"No."

"How'd you get him free? That thing could have taken off a finger!"

"I don't know!" Ellie cried. The more truth she swallowed, the bigger the lies she belched up. They were leaving a sour taste in her mouth. She couldn't believe her mother didn't smell them.

They drove down Second Street, turned right, and bumped across some railroad tracks before pulling into the vet's parking lot. Her mother leaned over the front seat. "Stay with Fang while I tell them we need help getting him in."

Ellie nodded.

She stroked Fang's head. "You're gonna be okay, boy."

Fang didn't open his eyes.

He's lost blood and he's in shock," Dr. Slight said as Ellie and her mother helped him carry Fang inside. "Leg looks pretty mangled." Walking backward, carrying the head of the stretcher, he led them into an operating room. They slid the stretcher onto a stainless steel table. "If you want to go home, I'd be happy to call you when I'm finished."

"I want to wait here," Ellie said.

"We'll wait for a while," Ellie's mother told him. "If we're gone, you'll know where to reach us."

"Help me get him off this, onto the table?" Dr. Slight asked. Fang slid off the stretcher easily. Ellie couldn't tell if he was breathing or not. "Would you call the dog's owner? No tags, but I believe he belongs to the Gordon family."

"I'll take care of that," her mother said, and with a touch to Ellie's cheek added, "and I'll call your father, too."

An hour later, Ellie and her mother were alone in the waiting room. Dr. Slight had sent his last two patients home. Her mother held Ellie's hand, stroking the top of it. Ellie was glad her mother wasn't trying to tell her everything would be okay. Fang had looked dead, lying on the stainless steel operating table. Nothing her mother could say would make what Ellie'd seen less bad.

The waiting room smelled like urine and disinfectant. It was a disgusting combination. Ellie would have preferred the smell of plain old pee.

And through a door behind the front desk came the muffled barking and whining of kenneled dogs. What really got her were the caged cats meowing. One of them sounded like Bob, begging to go outside.

The feeling came from nowhere—a sudden burst of anger at Bob for being so stupid, for wanting to go out so badly when he knew there were coyotes near the house. What did he expect a coyote to do?

In her anger Ellie tensed her hand, drew in her breath.

"Anything wrong, honey?" her mother asked.

Before she could say anything, the door opened and a man walked in.

"Mr. Gordon?" Ellie's mother asked, letting go of Ellie's hand and standing.

"Yes. Where's Sparky?"

"Sparky?"

The man nodded.

"An old dog, kind of a lab but more of a mutt, with some white around his muzzle?" asked Ellie's mother. "Sweet-tempered?"

"That's him," Mr. Gordon said.

"When he's around our house we call him Fang," her mother said.

"Fang?" The man looked puzzled. "Funny name," he said. He turned to look at Ellie. "Your mother said you found him in a trap?"

Ellie nodded.

The man shook his head. "Lordy!" he said. "That could make for a big bill. Look like he might have to amputate?"

Ellie nodded again. She hadn't thought about how much money this would cost. Should she pay?

"He's a sweet dog and Ellie here has grown quite fond of him," her mother was saying. "I'm just curious. Why do you let him wander so?"

"Just seemed cruel to lock him up," Mr. Gordon said. "Since our daughter, Molly, went off to college, he's taken to wandering. Always finds a place with a girl. You must remind him somehow of Molly," he said, looking at Ellie. He smiled at her, almost shyly. "I can see why."

"I'm sorry about what happened to him!" Ellie said. "I'll pay, or work for you."

Mr. Gordon shook his head. "Wasn't your fault, little lady. Guess we should have locked him up. Would have been less cruel than this."

Ellie opened her mouth to protest just as Dr. Slight came out of the operating room.

"Howdy, Gerald," he said, nodding to Mr. Gordon. He looked at Ellie. "He's going to be okay, thanks to you and your mother. Had to take off the leg, though. We'll keep him here

tonight and tomorrow to watch him, make sure everything is all right."

Fang was going to make it. But Ellie's eyes filled with tears. With only three legs, the old dog would probably stop wandering. She pictured him on the operating table. That was most likely the last time she'd ever see him.

Chapter 12

Troy had kept his distance from Ellie since the afternoon he stepped off the bus with her. Several kids, two boys in particular, had ribbed them both. Yesterday Troy was almost kicked off the bus for punching one of the boys when he asked how the honeymoon went. Ellie had just walked by.

This morning she would have risked all the kidding in the world to tell Troy about Fang and then rub his face in the whole bloody mess. But he was sitting in the back of the bus with Lester, and Beth was near the front.

"Troy gave this to me to give to you," Beth said as Ellie slid in beside her. Beth handed her a tiny lump of paper, so tightly folded Ellie couldn't help tearing it.

Checked the trap? the note said. There was a crude drawing of a skull and crossbones underneath.

"What does that mean?" Beth asked.

Ellie looked up, surprised that Beth had been reading over her shoulder. She was about to tell Beth to bug off, but thought better of it. "Troy set a trap near our house . . . a coyote trap."

"Oh." Beth hesitated. "Ellie. What's wrong?"

The story of the trap and Fang spilled out, along with a few angry tears Ellie couldn't stop.

As they got off the bus at school, Beth turned and glared in Troy's direction. "What a creep!" she said.

Ellie threw the note in a trash barrel.

■   ■   ■

Ellie called up the vet as soon as she got home that afternoon. Fang would be kept at the clinic for another day, Dr. Slight's assistant told her. He'd chewed on the bandage and torn out some stitches during the day. Otherwise, he was doing fine.

Ellie couldn't stop thinking about Fang and about what a coward she'd been, not owning up to her part in what had happened to him.

She had homework to do, but couldn't face it. She tried finishing the novel she'd been reading, but found herself flipping pages without understanding anything. She turned on the television, but her eyes kept shifting toward the window. The bright blue of the sky made the screen seem dull and lifeless. Thin clouds were stretched from one side of the window to the other. Ellie imagined that they were snagged on the mountains to the east and were being pulled thinner and thinner by westward winds. The more she watched, the more her insides threatened to snap like the clouds.

What was going on? She almost felt sick, but without the fever. She closed her eyes—and saw Fang as the trap snapped shut. Whenever she shifted her weight, the couch creaked, sounding like Fang as he'd hobbled back from the trap. She got up and began pacing the room.

The more she thought of Fang, the angrier she became at Troy. It had all been just a game with him. Anybody who knew anything would have known how dangerous traps are for animals besides coyotes. Ellie should have stopped him. He was nothing but a stupid kid, playing with life and death. If anybody should pay the vet bill, Troy should.

She clicked off the television and went outside. She didn't know exactly where she was headed until she found herself on the trail. The trap was luring her, as surely as if it held some powerful bait for her. Every once in a while she saw dark splotches on the trail that must have been Fang's blood.

The sprung trap was where it had landed the day before. Patches of dried blood were thick and smooth as fingernail polish. The dirt around it still looked torn and dark. Carefully, afraid that it could do further damage, Ellie carried the trap to a flat spot across the trail. Using a stick, she dug a hole to her wrists and buried it. She stomped and then scattered dirt over it.

There were still a couple of lumps of coyote scat off to the side of the trail. For a joke, she nudged them with her foot, pushing them onto the spot where the trap was buried. But the joke, she knew, wasn't on the coyote. The joke was on her and Troy and Fang. The coyote seemed cleverer by far than the rest of them put together. He'd eaten the bait without setting off the trap. He poked fun at them, dropping scat on the trap without setting it off or losing a foot or part of his tail. He'd spooked her so the first time that she'd looked for him in shadows where he hadn't been—or maybe he'd been so well hidden that she just hadn't seen him.

The coyote had made Troy and her look stupid. She couldn't help but admire that, and admiring the animal even just a little was making it difficult for her to keep focused on hating him.

She figured the only way to get even with a coyote was to become as clever as a coyote. And the only way to become clever was to know more about coyotes.

She pretended to walk back toward her house. Just out of sight of where the trap was buried, she looped back. She headed off the trail near the top of the ridge flank. Peeking over the top her eyes zoomed in on the coyote hole. She searched right and left to see if she was being spied on. All she saw was sky.

She watched the coyote hole for what seemed like a long time. As the sun moved, the den's mouth appeared to stretch sideways, grinning.

There was no movement from inside the den—no nose poking out, no eyes glinting.

Slowly, still not trusting that it might be empty, she crept forward. She stopped and listened. She heard nothing but the beat of blood in her ears. Had the coyote and his family been spooked enough to move—first by the setting of the trap and then by having Fang step into it? Dropping to her hands and knees, Ellie crawled forward.

She paused a few yards from the den and listened. Hearing nothing, she picked up a fist-sized rock and tossed it into the hole's mouth. Silence. She crawled even closer.

There were a few small bones scattered around the hole's lower lip. Maybe one of them was Bob's? A thin trail ran from the cave's mouth, reminding her of a string of dried spit on a kid's face. Off to the side were the tiny nubs of a backbone, delicate as strung pearls.

Peering inside, taking a deep breath, she thrust her head into the den.

Chapter 13

The entrance was barely large enough for her shoulders. The smell of pee grew more sour the deeper she crawled. Peering through the darkness, she tried to blink away the dust her hands and knees stirred. A fly bumped into her face. Her head scraped the ceiling and dirt crumbs fell down her collar. She tried to avoid touching hard things on the floor. Pebbles? Dried scat? More bones?

She stopped when her hands touched the back wall. In the dark it was difficult to know what she was smelling. Was this what it smelled like inside an animal skull, shreds of flesh and muscle and brains still clinging to it? She turned around slowly. The den opening looked as round as an empty eye socket.

Ellie sat on her haunches, her shoulders hunched against the ceiling, and let her thoughts fill the den. The quiet made the strange visions more vivid.

This was what a coyote pup saw, waiting for one of its parents to darken the hole. Would it be her mother, teats swelled with milk? Or her father with blood staining the fur around his mouth?

Ellie imagined coyote pups on the den's floor. How many were there? Were they stretching their legs, arching their backs? Were they wrestling with each other? Were they curled up asleep? Were they big enough to go outside? Images flashed through her head, answering these questions.

If coyote pups had been here, they were gone

now, big enough, perhaps, to eat meat. Had they helped themselves to parts of Bob? She felt numb more than angry thinking of coyote pups eating his flesh.

The den's opening stared at her, unblinking, and Ellie felt suddenly vulnerable. What would happen if a coyote came back to check on the den? Would it attack, knowing she couldn't escape?

Shaken by the thought of being trapped, she crawled to the den's opening and poked her head outside. She blinked at the sudden light, then squeezed her shoulders through. She emptied her lungs of the den's dark air and took a deep breath of brightness. The trapped feeling vanished.

After the quiet of the darkness, she heard sounds she hadn't noticed before—birds, wind through the trees. The hills seemed to keep a respectful distance but also seemed to protect. All eyes seemed to be on the den's opening, including the sun.

From this spot the coyotes had been able to see and hear most everything from all around without having to move. There weren't houses or cars or telephone poles. It was as if people didn't exist. Ellie felt the intelligence of this place, the beauty of it, the wisdom of digging a den here.

From beyond the ridge came the cry of a coyote. She recognized it. Her coyote. Had he moved his family beyond the ridge?

She was drawn toward the cry.

Beyond the ridge were many short, steep hills. The last was steepest, the dirt beneath her feet crumbly and coarse. Ellie took her time climbing it. She didn't want to spook them again.

She slowly raised her head above the hilltop. Not more than fifty yards away, on a steep south-facing hillside, she saw the opening to a den.

Ellie watched. She saw no movement and heard only an occasional bird call.

Suddenly, a face poked from the darkness and three fuzzy, round coyote pups tumbled from the den. Oddly, they were chocolate brown. Did their color stretch as they grew, thinning to the reddish, golden gray-brown of adult coyotes? Their ears were huge, almost catlike, and their eyes were large. Ellie watched one pup jump and pound and roll on another. The third pup batted at something on the ground. They were as cute as any puppy dogs she'd ever seen. Even as cute as kittens.

It took her a few moments to notice movement in the flat area above the hole, partly hidden by the thinning head of a piñon. A large coyote lifted its head. The mother?

A second adult appeared by the den opening, as if by magic. Another mother? It didn't seem big enough. An older sister or brother?

A third adult, beautifully tawny, approached the others. Ellie felt sure of it: This was the coyote she'd seen by her garage before and after Bob disappeared, the coyote who twice had looked down at her from the ridge.

The pups stopped playing and rushed to their father.

He stepped back, opened his mouth wide, seemed to curtsy while he dipped his head, and threw up. The pups leaped toward the slimy lumps that came from his mouth. The vomit looked like mice and one of the pups rolled in it. The father sat calmly, watching them eat.

His ears stiffened and he lifted his head. Ellie saw the two other adults raise their heads to look where he looked.

She dipped below the ridge, wanting not to be found out. Glancing at her watch, she saw it was getting late. Her father would be home soon. She was cutting it close.

She slipped down the hill and made her way toward the old den. She was just about there when she heard voices. Is that what the coyotes had heard long before she had? She couldn't make out the words.

Wary, she hid behind a large rock half buried by floodwaters roaring down in the arroyo. The voices grew louder.

"I tell you, it was in here somewhere."

Troy! She crouched, hoping to be as invisible as a coyote.

"Think you staked it good enough? Think there's a coyote around wearing chain jewelry?"

And Lester.

"I swear. I staked it good. You don't think wind could cover it up with dirt, do you?"

"Sure wouldn't want to step on it." Lester sounded unsure of himself.

Ellie smiled. Feeling like a coyote, liking the way it felt, she crept toward the edge of the rock, wanting a glimpse of the two boys pussyfooting around, afraid they were about to step on a trap.

"There's one way to spring it without stepping on it," Lester said. "You say it was right about here?"

BAM! The .22!

Ellie froze. Were they crazy?

BAM!

Troy and Lester laughed. "Not there. Or there."

"You sure nailed that stink bug!"

Lester laughed again. "Think Ellie took the trap?"

"Naw. There's a coyote around here she wants to kill."

Ellie flinched, remembering Fang when the trap snapped shut.

"This is stupid," Lester complained. "Trap could be anywhere. Want to check out that den near the arroyo with the wrecked car?"

"Sure," answered Troy. "It might have pups."

"Want to try snagging them?"

"Sure. How?" Their voices sounded as if they were walking away from her.

"Well, first you unravel some barbed wire and make hooks at the end of each strand. Then you stick it in the hole and jab around. Twist when it bumps into one of them. You snag them right under the hide and pull them out." Lester's voice was growing faint, but each word made Ellie wince. She pictured puppy shapes squealing and yelping, wire hooks cutting into their sides and chests and haunches. What if the wire poked one of them in the eye? Or in the mouth?

"Cool," she heard Troy say.

"Yep. Then you pop them on the head and fish out another one."

Ellie felt sick to her stomach. How could anybody do that—enjoy snagging pups like that?

A memory flicked into her brain.

She saw Bob walking into the house, something in his mouth. He set it at her feet: a dead baby rabbit missing one of its ears. "Shame on you!" she'd cried. But when she picked it up she realized the baby was still breathing.

Where had Bob gotten it? He was hurrying out the door and she followed him, catching a glimpse as he disappeared under a spirea bush. Setting the rabbit down, Ellie got on her hands and knees. She grabbed Bob by the scruff of the neck and pulled him out. In the hollow in the dirt she saw a nest of baby rabbits, all of them missing parts, all of them making hurt sounds.

Ellie closed her eyes against this memory. But she couldn't shut out the worst of it. She knew it would have been merciful to bash the babies in the head. That would have been quick, painless, sure. But instead of putting the baby rabbits out of their misery, she'd taken Bob inside and left them to die on their own.

She'd been no better than Bob. Or Troy or Lester. Worse even, because she'd put her own squeamishness ahead of what those baby rabbits were feeling, ignoring the fact that they'd die slowly, in pain.

She stepped from behind the boulder. Maybe

she could stop Troy and Lester from doing to the coyote pups what Bob had done to the baby rabbits.

She began to run, wanting to leave behind images of mangled rabbits, and wanting to catch up to Troy and Lester. She followed the dent of footprints in the arroyo sand until she heard their voices again. Gasping, she put on a burst of speed and was about to shout, when a *ka-bam!* shot down the arroyo as if through the barrel of a gun. Without hesitating, without thinking, her feet skipped and turned. Ellie sprinted, not knowing if she was running from the gun or toward home, hating Troy and Lester, but even more hating herself for being a coward.

Chapter 14

Ellie was late getting home. Late as she was, her father and mother were later. She paced through the house, trying to catch her breath, trying to calm her thoughts. But questions followed questions.

Where were her parents? Had Troy and Lester found the pups? Surely the gun had scared any coyotes all the way to Texas. Were her parents okay? What was going on?

She was just about to call the bank or the clinic, when she heard her father's truck pull up.

"Ellie!" he called from outside. Fearing the

worst, she ran out the kitchen door. Her father stood, grinning, by his truck.

The driver's side door was open. Something moved on the seat.

"Fang!" She rushed toward him and began to scramble up onto the seat.

"Steady." Her father put a hand on her shoulder. "We've got to be careful."

"How . . . ?"

"I called Mr. Gordon this afternoon," her father interrupted. "Asked if we could take care of him, since you're so fond of Fang and he's so fond of you. I told him you'd give the old fella the very best care, that maybe you could give him more time than the Gordons could, what with their jobs and all. And *ta-da!*'' He motioned toward Fang, as if he'd done a magic trick.

Ellie blinked, almost expecting Fang to disappear with a wave of her father's hand.

"Why don't you crawl up there, grab the other

end of the blanket, and help lift him out of the truck," he said.

As soon as they laid the blanket on the ground, Fang got up onto his legs. "Attaboy!" Ellie encouraged. She couldn't keep her eyes off his hindquarters. His left leg was gone. The white gauze bandage looked as if it were holding a small, round ham against his rear. What looked like ham juice was soaking through in spots. He was unsteady as he half-hopped and half-limped off the blanket on his single hind leg. He headed for the spirea bush. He stood for a moment, seeming to frown.

"I think he wants to lift his leg," said her father.

Ellie nodded. "Only he can't lift it with the other one chopped off."

She was about to go help Fang when he squared his shoulders and backed up, steering himself to the other side. He tipped slightly away from the bush, as if lifting an invisible leg. He did his thing and then came over to Ellie, lips raised in a smile. "Good boy!" She swallowed tears.

"Quite a dog," her father said.

Ellie knelt beside him and stroked his head. "You're a good dog, Fang." She looked at her dad. "Think we should call him Fang or Sparky?"

"Sparky doesn't fit," he replied. "Let me show you how to change the bandage."

Every afternoon that week Ellie rushed to get home to be with Fang. On Thursday Beth came with her. She and Beth spent nearly an hour in the backyard, throwing an old tennis ball for Fang to catch.

"I don't see how he does it," Beth said, when Fang began to tire.

"He's tough," Ellie said. He could run in a tight circle, jump some, and zigzag. The only way she knew he was tired was when his back hunched more than usual as he ran.

"He doesn't seem to feel sorry for himself."

"No," Ellie said. "I think I feel more sorry than he does. And sometimes J forget he only has three legs."

"Whatever happened to the trap?" Beth asked.

"Didn't I tell you?"

Beth shook her head.

"I buried it."

"It doesn't seem right, trying to kill a coyote like that." When Ellie was slow to respond, Beth continued. "I mean, the coyote was only trying to get something to eat. It's not like he was doing it for the fun of it."

"I bet he had fun." Ellie could almost taste the bitterness in her voice.

"Don't get sore." Beth's mouth was small and determined. "I'm just saying that Troy was doing it for fun and the coyote . . . *I* don't know! It's not like it was trying to hurt Bob. It was only trying to eat him."

Ellie felt the same frustration and confusion

she saw on Beth's face. How could you eat something without hurting it? She reached down and stroked Fang's head. "I don't know, either," she said. Coyotes had to eat—just like people. And eating meant killing. And it wasn't as if coyotes didn't enjoy hunting. Bob had enjoyed hunting mice and baby rabbits. Sometimes he'd eaten them and sometimes he hadn't. With coyotes it was simpler than that. If they didn't eat what they caught, they might starve—or have to eat apples.

Gravel crunched as a car came up their driveway. Beth looked at her watch. "My mom," she said, getting up.

"Call me later?"

"Yeah . . . sure."

Ellie woke the next morning confused and exhausted. All night her head had been filled with cartoon sound effects. Dynamite exploding.

Whistling sounds going from high to low as a cartoon coyote fell from bridges and cliffs or was shot into the air with rockets strapped to his back. Beep-beeping as a roadrunner zipped by. Thumps as rocks and anvils fell to squash the coyote. Accordion sounds as he walked away from the spot where he'd been smashed flat.

Just like the cartoon, it had been one thing after another, the stunts getting fancier and the coyote losing more and more dramatically.

And then, just before she woke, the situation changed: the coyote had his prey dangling in his hand by the neck. He was looking the roadrunner in the eye . . . was opening his toothy mouth. . . . Slowly, he closed it, seeming more defeated than ever.

Why? Why hadn't the coyote eaten the road-runner? Why had he suddenly plunked him down, let him go?

When she woke, she was too troubled by her dream to fall back to sleep. She watched the light growing stronger in her room, wanting the dream's meaning to dawn on her. She listened to sounds coming in from her open window and wanted to hear coyotes, but didn't. She got up, careful not to disturb Fang, who was occupying most of her bed. She dressed quietly and padded to the kitchen in bare feet.

She fixed a bowl of cereal and began to eat mechanically, chewing each mouthful so much there was almost nothing to swallow.

What would she have done if she'd gone to the trap and found a coyote caught in it, alive? Would she have left it to die? Would she have called Troy and Lester to kill it?

If she'd had a gun, would she have pulled the trigger herself?

What if she'd wanted to set it free? Would it have allowed her to come near?

Standing, she rinsed her cereal bowl, feeling as tired and defeated as the cartoon coyote letting the roadrunner go. Beth had tried to put this confusion into words and couldn't. Had chasing after the roadrunner been more important to the coyote than catching it?

On her way to the refrigerator for lunch things, she glanced at the fishbowl. The fish was floating and had lost its color.

She plucked the fish out and held it in the palm of her hand. She remembered it blowing kisses to the motorboat fly. She pictured it drawing closer and closer to Bob's tongue lapping water.

She glanced at the shamrocks. A couple of leaves were pushing up, still folded tight as umbrellas. Her mother had put aluminum foil around the pot a couple of days ago and it had worked, keeping the mice away.

She heard dog toenails approaching from the living room. Quickly, she stuck a finger in the shamrock's dirt, next to where she remembered dropping the fly, and wiggled it, making the hole bigger. She dropped in the fish and covered it up.

Turning around, she smiled through her tears. "How are you doing?" she asked. "How'd you sleep?"

His tail wagged, answering both of her questions, almost toppling him.

Chapter 15

I'm home!" Ellie called as she burst into the kitchen. "All-ee, all-ee, in come free!"

She was getting used to Fang greeting her, as enthusiastic as if she'd come home from landing on the moon. But this afternoon the silence in the house was confusing. Where was that happy yelp, the thump as he jumped off her bed, the skittering of dog claws on the floor as he raced toward her?

She rushed to her bedroom. He wasn't on her bed. She searched the house, growing frantic with worry. Had something happened to him?

She grabbed her phone and dialed her father's number.

"Hello?"

"Dad!"

"Hi, Ellie." He sounded as if his thoughts were elsewhere. "I'm in a meeting right now. Can I call you later?"

"No!" she cried. "Fang's not here! Did you take him back to the vet? Did Mr. Gordon take him back?"

"No. He should be there." She had his full attention now.

"Well, he's not!" she panted, her chest tight, feeling as if she'd run a mile.

"Oh, shoot!" She heard her father's muffled voice telling whoever was in his office to excuse him for a moment. "Ellie? You there? I let him out this morning to do his thing, and I forgot to let him back inside!"

■   ■   ■

Ellie ran past the garage, calling his name every few steps. "Fang! Fang! FANG!" She stopped and looked around, wanting not to move so fast that Fang wouldn't be able to catch up if he heard her.

She looked toward the ridge, scouring it with her eyes. Had coyotes seen Fang's injury? Had they lured him into the hills so they could ambush him?—kill him?—eat him?

She ran along the coyote trail, dodging the branches of piñon and juniper trees. She didn't have spare breath to call his name. She was nearing the spot where the first trap had been set and was running so fast that she almost stepped in another one.

She leaped over it and skidded to a stop. A raven cawed and flapped away from her, so close she felt the breeze of its wings.

The trap was set. Near it were pieces of hot dog. Ellie looked from it to the raven, which had settled on a large rock a few yards away. Its head was cocked, making it look as if it were keeping one eye on her and the other on the pieces of hot dog.

Ellie's heart was pounding and her hands shook. "You want it?" she asked the raven, her voice thin and wobbly.

She grabbed a stick by her feet that was as long as her arm and stabbed at the trap's tongue. She kept her distance, treating the trap as if it were a live thing, and missed twice. On the third jab, the trap leaped, snapping shut on the stick. She gasped and the stick flew from her hands as if the trap had pulled it from her.

The raven hesitated only a moment before hopping down, snatching a piece of hot dog from the ground, and flying to the top of a piñon tree.

The trap lay like a dead thing, the stick clenched in its teeth. Ellie carefully picked it up. Its chain tether led her to the stake, which she yanked free. Was this the same trap she'd buried? She walked to where she thought the first trap was and kicked at it with her heel. After a few strikes, she saw the shape of its wings emerging from the powdery dirt.

Somebody had put a second trap in this place. Troy?

Anger swelled in her gut. She should have told him. Surely he wouldn't have set another trap if he'd known what the first one had done to Fang.

Or would he?

Her hands tightened into fists. From the corner of her eyes she saw a hunched and hobbling form hop-walk toward her.

"Fang!"

He tucked his head lower, walked next to her, and sat. His tongue hung from the side of his mouth and he smiled up at her.

"You crazy, wonderful dog, you!" Ellie cried, dropping to her knees and hugging him. "Oh, Fang!" He snuffed around her neck and licked her ear. Ellie laughed at the way it tickled.

"Come on, fella," she said, getting up. She picked up the trap she'd buried and the second trap by the stick held in its jaws. "Let's go home."

Her father was outside, calling for Fang and for her.

"We're here!" she called back.

He rushed up to them. "Ellie!" His eyes kept flicking from Ellie to Fang and back again. "Where'd you find him?"

"Out beyond the ridge—" she began.

"Where did those come from?" he asked, his eyes narrowing.

She held out the stickless trap. "Here's the one that got Fang." The chain rattled from the trap on the stick. "I sprung this just a little while ago."

Her father looked at the traps, shaking his head.

Ellie hesitated. She was responsible for this second trap herself, just as surely as she'd helped Troy set the first trap. She saw questions in her father's eyes. Scared as she was to give him the answers, she wanted to. The secrets had grown too big to keep inside anymore. "Daddy?"

He nodded.

"Could you drive me into town? In a couple of minutes?"

He nodded again.

"I . . . we can talk on the way there. But first, I need to use the phone."

Ellie dropped the traps by the steps and went in to the phone. She picked up the phone book and, before she opened it, was surprised to realize she knew Troy's number by heart.

Punching the keypad calmed her. She breathed evenly, deeply, as she listened to the distant ringing. She knew what she had to say, but didn't know how she would say it. She wanted to let him have it, to let her words go through him like bullets. She also knew she'd be riding in a school bus with him for many years. Could she be brutally honest and careful at the same time?

"Troy?"

She hadn't expected him to answer the phone. Her tongue stiffened as she opened her mouth. But words rolled off it like gum balls from a roundheaded machine "We've gotta talk. Now. My dad will drive me. I'll be there in fifteen minutes."

She set the phone down. This much she knew: Troy was going to know everything. And he was going to help pay for what happened to Fang. And he could arrange all that with Lester any way he wanted.

Chapter 16

Moonlight poured into her bedroom. Ellie lifted her hand toward the window. She wouldn't have been surprised to feel it slip through skin and bone—cool as water but ghostly.

The moon was nearly full and Fang was restless. Ellie lowered her hand and looked out at the nearly transparent landscape. The moon seemed to light up the part of her thoughts that remembered Bob.

Fang lifted his head. This was his last night with her for a while. Molly was coming home from college for spring break. She peeled back the bedcovers. "Go outside?" she asked.

Moonlight made the Bob of her memory appear silvery. The air was filled with the scent of lilacs. He had loved that bush. She walked past it toward the crab-apple tree, which was also in bloom. He had loved climbing it—once stranding himself on a top branch. Ellie had rescued him by climbing up with her backpack, stuffing him inside as he hissed and scratched.

Off in the distance, she heard a sound like coyotes running through an arroyo or along a ridge. Coyotes or a breeze rounding the garage? The breeze was too gentle.

She and Fang walked beyond the garage and heard it again. What were the coyotes chasing? Or were they just singing? The sound no longer made her tremble.

Lately, she'd heard her coyote—Bob's coyote—

almost every morning. Not far but not too close. Sometimes she didn't realize she'd heard his cry until later—at breakfast or while combing her hair.

Ellie heard Bob's meow in his bark so clearly that her chest ached, seeming to swell. She wanted to call back. She wanted to answer Bob—to tell him that she loved him, that everything would be all right. She wanted to answer the coyote—to tell him she was stronger than he thought, stronger and wiser. She lifted her face to the moon, wanting to howl, to make the moon shiver with the pleasure of fear, with the beauty of her sadness.

The sound that came out of her mouth was more of a belch than a howl, stretching upward from the root of her throat. Fang joined in, his cry like a breezy gust, whisking her sound toward the moon, stretching it thinner, making it beautiful.

The coyote replied, seeming respectful, careful.

Moonlight glinted off a tear poised to fall. After a few moments, it streaked down her face. A corner of her smile caught it.